Dear Parent:

Congratulations! Your child is taking the first steps on an exciting journey. The destination? Independent reading!

STEP INTO READING® will help your child get there. The program offers five steps to reading success. Each step includes fun stories and colorful art. There are also Step into Reading Sticker Books, Step into Reading Math Readers, Step into Reading Write-In Readers, Step into Reading Phonics Readers, and Step into Reading Phonics First Steps! Boxed Sets—a complete literacy program with something for every child.

Learning to Read, Step by Step!

Ready to Read Preschool–Kindergarten
• big type and easy words • rhyme and rhythm • picture clues
For children who know the alphabet and are eager to begin reading.

Reading with Help Preschool–Grade 1
• basic vocabulary • short sentences • simple stories
For children who recognize familiar words and sound out new words with help.

Reading on Your Own Grades 1–3
• engaging characters • easy-to-follow plots • popular topics
For children who are ready to read on their own.

Reading Paragraphs Grades 2–3
• challenging vocabulary • short paragraphs • exciting stories
For newly independent readers who read simple sentences with confidence.

Ready for Chapters Grades 2–4
• chapters • longer paragraphs • full-color art
For children who want to take the plunge into chapter books but still like colorful pictures.

STEP INTO READING® is designed to give every child a successful reading experience. The grade levels are only guides. Children can progress through the steps at their own speed, developing confidence in their reading, no matter what their grade.

Remember, a lifetime love of reading starts with a single step!

Step into Reading, Random House, and the Random House colophon are registered
trademarks of Random House, Inc.

Visit us on the Web!
www.stepintoreading.com
www.randomhouse.com/kids

Educators and librarians, for a variety of teaching tools, visit us at
www.randomhouse.com/teachers

Library of Congress Cataloging-in-Publication Data
Harper, Benjamin.
Going bananas / by Benjamin Harper;
illustrated by Erik Doescher, Mike DeCarlo, and David Tanguay
     p. cm. — (Step into reading. A step 2 book)
"DC Super Friends."
Summary: When a priceless yellow diamond is stolen from the museum, Superman,
Batman, and the other Super Friends follow the clues and discover that Gorilla Grodd is
using the diamond to create an army of yellow gorillas.
ISBN 978-0-375-85613-6 (trade pb) — ISBN 978-0-375-95613-3 (lib bdg.)
[1. Superheroes—Fiction.] I. Doescher, Erik, ill. II. DeCarlo, Mike, ill. III. Tanguay, David,
ill. IV. Title.
PZ7.H231315 Go 2009 [E]—dc22 2009004878

Printed in the United States of America
20 19 18 17 16 15 14

Everyone wants to see the big yellow diamond!

The diamond is gone!
Without it,
the show cannot open.

The Super Friends
will help!
They will find
the diamond.

Superman uses
his X-ray vision.
He finds a clue!

Green Lantern
finds another clue!
He spots
strange fingerprints.

Across town,
there is trouble
at the docks.

All the bananas are gone!
Batman, Robin,
and the Flash
are ready to help.

Batman spots
more strange
fingerprints!

Superman sees
more trouble.
A truck full of bananas
has been stolen!

Superman follows
the truck.
It races
down the city streets.

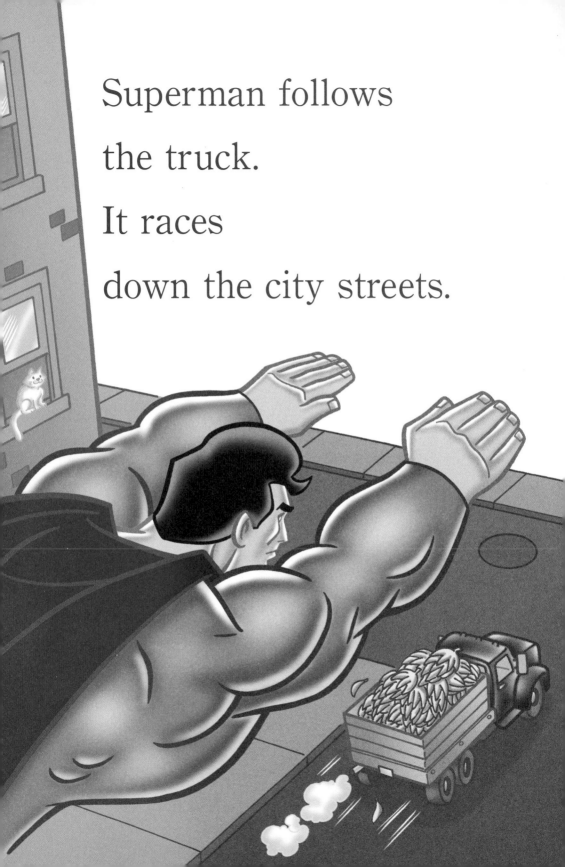

The truck stops.

A gorilla gets out!

Superman takes

a closer look.

It is Gorilla Grodd!
He is using a magic box,
the diamond, and
the bananas.

He is making
a magic
gorilla army.

"You are too late!"
Grodd says.

"My gorillas will
take over the city.
And then we will
take over the world!"

Gorillas go everywhere!

They run in the park.

They jump into the pond.

The Flash ties up

a gorilla

with rope!

Cyborg helps.

Gorillas run wild!

They make a mess.

Robin and Green Lantern
trap the gorillas.
They cannot go
anywhere!

Superman works fast.

The gorillas turn back
into bananas!

Batman captures Grodd!

25

Roar!

Grodd breaks free.

He grabs the diamond.

He escapes!

Superman chases Grodd.

He must not get away!

Gorilla Grodd hides
at the zoo.
Which gorilla has
the diamond?

Superman knows!

Growl!

Gorilla Grodd cannot
hide anymore.

He is taken away.

The Super Friends
return the diamond
just in time.
The show can go on.

The gem show is a hit—
thanks to
the Super Friends!